Honey, Honey

Written by Jo Windsor
Illustrated by Richard Hoit

Rigby

The bears went
down the steps.

The bears went
along the path.

The bears went
over the bridge.

4

The bears went
across the tree.

The bears went across the tree.

The bears went
over the bridge.

The bears went
along the path.

The bears went
up the steps.

Guide Notes

Title: Honey, Honey
Stage: Emergent – Magenta

Genre: Fiction
Approach: Guided Reading
Processes: Thinking Critically, Exploring Language, Processing Information
Visual Focus: Trail
Word Count: 48

READING THE TEXT

Tell the children that the story is about two bears who are looking for some honey to eat.
Talk to them about what is on the front cover. Read the title and the author / illustrator.
"Walk" through the book, focusing on the illustrations and talking to the children about
where the bears are going on their way to get the honey. Talk about what happens to
the bears when they find the honey.
Before looking at pages 12 - 13, ask the children to make a prediction.
Read the text together.

THINKING CRITICALLY
(sample questions)
- What do you think the bears had to eat jam?
- What do you think the bears will do next time they want some honey?

EXPLORING LANGUAGE

Terminology
Title, cover, author, illustrator, illustrations

Vocabulary
Interest words: bears, steps, path, bridge, tree, honey
High-frequency words: the, went
Positional words: down, over, up, across, along

Print Conventions
Capital letter for sentence beginnings, periods